GW01316390

A Gathering Of Grim Stori[

Iris Lloyd is a ten year old writer and illustrator from London and this is her first publication. She has written and edited the 6 short stories held within the covers of this book on her own. Much of the editing was completed by Iris during and after the school day with a little guidance from her Year 5 teacher and her family. The illustrations are Iris's own drawings, scanned by Iris in school and edited with photo editing software with the help of a graphic designer.

First published in Great Britain in 2015

This book has been written and illustrated by Iris Lloyd

Edited by Iris Lloyd with a little help from school and home

Illustrations edited for book use by Nick Parsons

Foreword written by Tom Percival, illustrator of Skulduggery Pleasant and author of Jack's Amazing Shadow

Copyright © July 2015 by Iris Lloyd

Foreword

My name is Tom Percival. I work as an author/illustrator, my most well-known work is probably the Skulduggery Pleasant book cover illustrations.

Last week a friend of mine emailed me to ask if I would write a foreword for a collection of stories by a pupil of his who is still at primary school.

I know first-hand how important a word of encouragement at the right time can be, so I said that I'd have a look over the stories, but I needed to clear some of my work away first.

I then made a cup of coffee and decided to have a quick flick through the stories before I got back on with my work....

I didn't stop until I had read them all.

I had expected to read them and to offer some support and encouragement, but what I hadn't expected was to be so utterly transported.

My own work remained uncompleted as I tore through this collection. The inventiveness, atmosphere and drama in Iris' work is staggering, and I was immediately transported into the strange and macabre worlds that you too are about to enter.

I could make more of a point of Iris's age, but that would be an insult to her obvious talent - Iris is not just a talented young author - she is a talented author - and I wish her the best of luck*

*Unless we ever have books released simultaneously, in case hers sold better **

** That's a joke, I'm not quite that embittered by the world, not yet anyway!

Tom Percival. July 2015

Thank you to my Mum, Dad, sister Kleio, Panda and my two cheeky cats Sooty and Timmy. Also to Dan for helping me so much

Contents

Dark streets

Dark streets

Edith, the petrified maid of Lord and Lady Neville, ran through the dark, cobbled streets, her boots splashing in the murky puddles as her heavy steps echoed around the town. She'd only set out for the night's usual errands, fetching the wet nurse and such like, but it was pitch black, cold and late, and something was wrong. Very wrong. Edith's main priority was survival, not the wet nurse. Well, at least she was good with the survival part - she'd been living with next to nothing all her life. She was tired, and it took all her will to stop herself slumping against the brick walls of the huge, looming houses that she zoomed past.

The many inhabitants of the town were asleep, snuggled up in their expensive eiderdown quilts, warm in their cosy homes, but Edith was awake. The rain flew down in swarms of angry bees, heading towards the pavement, soaking Edith to the bone. She shook her head dizzily, trying to see if it was still following her. She looked in every corner, desperately trying to find an alleyway to hide in. Whipping her straggly hair out of the way, she could hear it coming, closing in on her, closer and closer, coming to end her life...she shook her head. It had to be a nightmare...or was it?

Fat, hot tears cascaded down her cheeks, spurring her onwards. Suddenly, she saw it. A place to hide. But she had to be quick, so she hastily threw herself into the dark alleyway hoping that someone, in some way, would save her, and tell her it was all okay. She closed her eyes, trying to get herself away from it, even for only a second. She held her breath, wishing that she was in the warm arms of safety.

Then she heard it, the noise that made her heart jolt. A rasping, rattling whisper, that however quiet, rang around the alleyway so loud it could shatter glass. She opened her eyes and felt glued to the spot. She could not look away from it, however hard she tried. As she cowered away into a small bundle on the damp pavement, Edith was paralysed with fear. It came closer and closer, its satisfied breath reaching out into the night. It was so close. Looming over her, the creature's eyes blazing neon yellow; she knew that there was only one thing that she could do now to save herself. At first nothing came out of her mouth, but then she realised it was her last chance, and she screamed, her shoulders heaving with fear as she trembled and whimpered, yelling for her life.

"Help! HELP!!!" she sobbed, hoping that someone would hear her cries. The creature stopped leaning forwards, and just stood there, its eyes glaring hatred and evil right into Edith's. A fanged, sly grin was stretched across its face as Edith shouted and cried, until her throat was hoarse and she could cry no longer. Then, when all was silent, the monster began creeping closer again. She closed her eyes tight, believing that now there was no way out. She took a shaky breath, knowing that it was to be her last.

She was ready to hand over her life to the beast that was tormenting her. But suddenly, a warm orange glow seemed to radiate out of the darkness. The monster narrowed its eyes, gasped and squealed, then backed away fast and seemed to melt into the darkness of the night, gone in a second. She looked with the last of her strength to the source of the light, and she could just make out a fuzzy silhouette of a woman, hobbling quickly towards her from a doorway. She smiled a relieved smile and fell stone cold, but not quite dead, on the floor.

A gentle hand shook her, and suddenly Edith awoke. She was surprised to see she was in a bed, and in the warmth of a room with the same orange light pulsing from a thick dribbling candle. "What...where am I?" she began trying to sit up, with a deeply confused look on her face, but she was interrupted by a woman with kind, smiling eyes seated near her bed. "John! She's awake!" she called excitedly. A middle-aged man with a fuzzy brown beard, which had patches of silver growing up the edges, stumbled into the room.
"She is? She is! Oh, I thought she never would wake!" he exclaimed excitedly.
Edith frowned. "Where is it...?" she mumbled in a confused manner, her eyes darting around the crumbling but cosy room, unsure about what was happening or where she was.

"Where is who, dear?" the woman asked, worriedly staring into Edith's eyes.

"The – The monster!" Edith stuttered.

"Darling, what monster?" the concerned woman asked again. Edith did not answer.

"Mary dear, she's most probably delirious - little servants like her often do end up getting a knock to the head and -"

"Shhh, John! I tell you she IS awake, and I can pretty much tell that she is telling the truth. Just look at her eyes, the poor lamb is petrified by whatever she saw. Maybe she is being punished by her master and needs a place to stay!" Mary suggested firmly.

"It's coming..." Edith muttered weakly, and then began to let the bottled up tears run.

"Oh don't cry dear! Maybe, John, you are right after all, my love. We didn't see no monster out there...yes, she's probably just a little bit sickly from the freezing cold, and she must be hungry...John!" she called.

"Yes, dear?" echoed a voice from the rickety old kitchen.

"Get the poor little girl a hot mug of tea will you?" she asked, and after a little while, John brought in a steaming mug of tea and placed it on the bedside table.

"Drink it while it's hot dear," smiled Mary. Edith gingerly sipped at the tea and savoured its warming embrace, the rosiness returning to the apples of her cheeks.

"So dear, tell us about this "monster" of yours." she said, obviously not believing Edith. The girl was just about to tell her the story when something caught her eye by the window. She stared in utter disbelief. There, tapping at the window was none other than the same slithering creature. It stood sickeningly at the front door, staring through the glass of the window, taunting the terrified maid once more and freezing Edith to the bone. "It's there...!" she screamed, raising a shaky finger to the door. The beast smiled in the direction of the terrified maid as the door knob started to turn...

The face in the picture

The face in the picture

Isla was fourteen. She deserved a life of excitement and adventure, but instead she was stuck in a room. A room that was blindingly white, almost like snow on a sunny day. It was also very, very bland. Completely undecorated, apart from a ragged black and white photo hanging lifelessly from the wall. It seemed to not really belong in the room - even its own plastic frame looked out of place. It showed a scene of a busy market place, bustling and exciting. It would be completely normal except for just for one, exquisite detail. All the faces of the people were facing towards you, eternally looking at you, never letting you slip out of their gripping stare. It felt like a million forced smiles were upon their faces and it looked spookily unnatural. Something was dangerously wrong with this picture, but Isla didn't see it. She just occasionally glanced at it, never giving it a second thought. It was just one picture out of a world of others, she thought. Nothing was wrong with it. Well, that was where she was fatally wrong.

There was one source of light in this room and it came from the window. At night, darkness would grasp the room in its unforgiving hand and all hope would dissolve. But now it was light, and Isla could do nothing but stare through the cold metal bars of the window at the heavily drizzling rain, pitter-pattering in time to her melancholy beating heart.

Her eyelids drooped and she felt as if all excitement had left her and only flecks of uninspiring boredom were hanging lonely in the emptiness of her head, knowing that they were deeply unwanted. The rain almost drove her mad. The repetitive drill and drone of it over and over, and although she'd only been in there a matter of moments, it felt as though it had been a life time. The rain's monotonous vibrating battered into her head, it seemed almost like she'd known it all her life. She said nothing, but inside she felt as if she was about to go round the bend.

Suddenly, her blood froze. She could feel a rattling breath on her neck. Isla's heart was in her mouth. She almost daren't look behind her shoulder. ALMOST. She gulped, then, trembling, she slowly turned her horror stricken head. She found herself face to face with Death himself.

She was paralysed. Fear flooded her, and she could not speak. He was just a skeleton, no eyes, only merciless dark sockets. He wore a long black cloak that was whispering and rustling slowly in the breeze. Was this a sick joke her parents had played on her? But the real feeling of eeriness occurred when she followed her curious gaze to the staff he was holding. As her eyes met the rusty wooden handle, she knew it was going to be bad. She found herself staring at a long crooked blade, sprinkled with sparkling crimson blood, shining and shimmering in the grey daylight.

She could do nothing. She couldn't run away, and she most definitely could not scream. Even if she did, where would she go? And who would hear her? She was alone in the locked up house.

'I am Death...' a shaky and sinister voice whispered. The very sound sent chills flying down her spine. She nodded, and she felt that she was now confident, because the deafening silence had been broken. The skull, which up until now had been emotionless, displayed a demonic smile. He held out a bony hand.

'You must not be afraid of me' he drawled. Isla could not look away out of morbid fascination. She was entranced.

'I can grant you your heart's desire...' he bribed.

'Tell me it – it *WILL* come true…' Isla reached out a gingerly, shaking hand and felt his. It was cold and raspy, and she immediately recoiled. Death didn't seem to mind. He knew the pact had been sealed now.

'I… I… ' She looked around the room. What was her heart's desire? She couldn't think. Suddenly, the haunting photo caught her eye. Death grinned. He had always known what she wanted.

Finally, Isla spoke. 'Err… I want to… Go back in time.' she stuttered doubtfully.
Hastily, Death replied in a whisper 'Your wish shall be granted.' he whispered before Isla could change her mind. Then a dark, swirling void took control of Isla. She felt as if she was dying. She closed her heavy eyelids, knowing that it was over, and she was stupid to even think that Death would save her. At once she could tell something was wrong.

It was a while before the horrible truth dawned on her. She was stuck inside the photo. From behind the plastic frame covering the picture, she found she was looking out onto the bleak room from where she had once stood. Death was hovering in a disgustingly evil manner below the picture that Isla was cruelly held captive inside. She was left speechless. However hard she tried, she could not speak anyway.

Death had tricked her, and there was nothing she could do about it. She looked around herself, and in her complete horror, she saw that instead of earth's colours, the world in the photo was just black and white. None of the enchanting colours of the rainbow shone, and horror stricken, Isla looked to her mortal hands. They too were drained of colour. She tried to scream, but nothing escaped her mouth. It was like a nightmare, but she knew she could never wake up to the real world. The people in the picture seemed to be moving, and they were all staring out towards the white room, as if posing for a photo. But if Isla looked closer, she could see the people's mouths moved without a sound. She read their lips: 'Help me... ' they repeated over and over, but silence was all that came out. Isla tried to back away, but she hit the hard plastic of the frame of the photo. She whipped her head around and tried to signal to Death but his fingers just clicked in a ghastly goodbye, and in a twist of spiralling black smoke, he disappeared.

Dylan was a cheery chap. A boy of fifteen; he entered the blank room. A photo caught his eye. It made him stare. It showed a bustling Victorian scene, and in the direct centre stood a teenage girl dressed in curiously modern clothing. A forced smile was reflected on a ghostly face. A single nameplate was below her. In gold italics, it spelled '*ISLA*'. Dylan frowned. He was sure he had heard that name before. He looked more closely at the girl's face and he saw a fat, hot tear roll down her cheek…

Banshee the troublesome cat

Banshee the troublesome cat

Banshee ran like she'd never run again. She was being ambushed by a clan of he-cats. She opened her mouth, letting her scent glands smell the bitter air. Her territory was close. Just a few more yards and she'd be safe. 'Back off, you mouse brains!' gasped Banshee as she elegantly leaped over a gnarled tree-root that was the beginning of her territory. She jumped gracefully into her den, her heart pounding strongly. She knew she was safe, as every cat knows, it is forbidden to be caught on another's patch. She caught her precious breath, and settled into her small patch of dry, flattened and prickly hay. 'That was close, they could've got you! You shouldn't explore so much!' she grumbled to herself as she, still trembling, licked the wounds on her back leg. There were beads of scarlet blood trickling down her bendy back. The next morning she woke up early, her shiny blue eyes expecting an unwanted visitor. 'No rats today,' she mewed quickly to herself as she cautiously padded out of her hiding place. She kept to the shadows, still expecting a growl from the bushes, or a shudder from the trees.

She sighed- a sigh of relief, her walk slowed and became more relaxed. She spotted the open fence of the garden, which had recently been removed and now left a gaping hole between the trees exposing the gardens, which were normally off limits.

Burning with uncontrollable curiosity, she found herself almost running towards the nearest garden. She padded silently through the ornamental statues and brightly coloured gnomes. But amongst the neat flowerbeds and newly mown grass, she could smell old fox scents in the air, stale and stinking. There was a small hole in the fence, and she easily slipped through it. She was suddenly overwhelmed by foul-smelling fumes: pollution gushing through her delicate nostrils, she stepped back, and slowly opened her eyes to a busy road, engulfed in the horrid stench of petrol. Cars were noisily zooming past, leaving a visible trail of thick smoke. She patiently waited for a gap wide enough to slip in between the travelling vehicles. She grew impatient, and when she thought they would never stop, she leapt across the dangerous road like a tiger hunting its prey, totally unaware of the danger, as a huge white truck almost ran her over. Once she at last reached the other side of the street, where safety engulfed her once more, she let out an angry hiss 'Rats! What a risk!' she spat.

With that, she slunk down the cobbled street, her elegant lynx-like markings turning everyone's heads. 'Wow Mummy! That cat looks like a leopard!' chimed some five-year-old twins to their mother, pointing their chubby fingers at Banshee.

Banshee proudly swaggered down the street, leading to a filthy alleyway. She shuddered as she entered the thin street, the cobbles were strewn with beer cans and half-eaten pizzas. A clump of scary-looking men were smoking in a corner. 'Uh oh!' gulped Banshee but she confidently strode forward, trying to look threatening. The men cackled, and the fattest man, covered in disgusting tattoos, lumbered towards her. 'Go away, you big thug!' she hissed but it made no difference.

She was forced back into a corner, as there was nowhere else to go. Before she knew it, the leader of the gang had staggered forward, and held her by the scruff of her neck with his rough and worn hands, and whispered threateningly into her ear, 'Hello pussy, you're a stray aren't ye?" he snarled, whilst his gang laughed loudly, taking big gulps of beer.

'Let's take this little kitty where she belongs. In the bin!' He cackled, holding the kicking and scratching cat, he walked towards to a large wheelie-bin.

'N! Nooo!' mewed Banshee as she was violently thrown into the bin, and was plunged into darkness. She yowled till her tiny lungs were sore but it was no use, as nobody would hear her screams. The bin lid closed with a thump.

There was no point struggling, she thought, and so settled down to sleep, curled uncomfortably amongst the bin bags and half-recognisable, food oozing out pus. "Anyway," she thought, "the bin men have to open this bin some day, and I'll be out of here in a flash."

She was rudely awoken some time later by light flooding into the bin. A friendly face came into view, and a posh lady's voice rang out. 'Oh my!' she exclaimed loudly. 'John! John! Come look, a cat in the bin!' she squealed, cupping her hands around her mouth.

A weedy man with large glasses carefully lifted her out with gentle and trembling hands. 'Oh my gosh, she must be a stray- what on earth is that stench?! We should take her to a cat's home,' he announced, producing a large cage from a nearby house.

Soon, after much fighting and struggling, Banshee was whisked off to a cat's home with her defeated head hung low, scared by this metal contraption she was being imprisoned inside. It smelled very strongly of soap and toilet disinfectant. The minutes rolled by for Banshee in her very badly chosen cage, and it wasn't long before she was taken to a tall looming building. As soon as she had passed the gates, she knew exactly where she was. This was the place every cat hated more than anything in the world-it was the cattery. She started to hiss and yowl uncontrollably, and so her imprisoners threw a towel over her cage. This is where all cats were humiliated and disgustingly over fed, and groomed until all their fur would fall out. She was immediately pushed into a cage with her old friend Toya- Cleopatra, the famous she-cat. She pierced Banshee with such a look that made Banshee wince, then went back to her washing, without a word. After a long, awkward silence Banshee casually asked, 'So, er, how did you get here?' and prowled up to the bored cat.

'I explored a school, got kicked out, and ended up here. What about you?' She looked up, and gave an unexpected friendly smile.

'Oh, I went into town and got found by a lady who brought me here. So should we sleep?' she suggested, trying not to mention the whole accident with the bin. She had just become very conscious of her very rotten smelling odour and was trying desperately to not let on. Banshee's cellmate, Toya was almost like the queen of all cats, and no one liked to seem below her. Banshee suddenly seemed very tired and put all thoughts of her own personal hygiene to one side.

'Um, do you want to go to sleep, then?' asked Banshee cautiously, worrying that the cat would catch on to her unpleasant pong if she was conscious any longer.

'I guess so...' mumbled Toya, lumbering sleepily towards a small cat-bed.

They awoke to the sound of rattling food falling into a metal cat bowl. Banshee wasn't used to kitty-pet ways and cautiously approached the bowl, padding it carefully with one paw. Toya yowled in laughter as she tucked into her canned dinner, lacking any knowledge of manners.

Later on that day, a beautiful young girl, probably aged 12, who both cats agreed, looked like a warrior princess, entered the cats' home. Her dad guided her through the millions of cats: fluffy ones, skinny ones, fierce ones, cute ones, but she didn't like any of them until she came to Banshee's cage. 'Oh, she's beautiful dad!' breathed the girl as she stroked Banshee's silky muzzle. 'I'm getting her!' announced the girl proudly, as she opened the cage to take her home. Banshee had thought that she'd hate this strange girl, and having to live as a pet, but somehow, she liked her. Maybe, Banshee thought, I won't mind this girl that much after all, she thought contently as the girl stroked her gently on the neck.

A pauper's story

A pauper's story

A loud knock came at the Saddlewick family's door.

"Go an get it, will ya?" a tired Mrs Saddlewick yelled from the busy kitchen as she tended to five year old Margaret and young Albert, whilst Amelie and James had an argument about who went to the door first as Sandra and Elizabeth played with their dolls. In the end, James won and proudly creaked open the sticky door cautiously. Standing there was a pale young woman, her dark brown hair straggly and long around her sweating face. She stood in the dark autumn night, her feet sore after boring a clear path through the millions of fallen amber crunching leaves.

As James's puzzled gaze fell on the swelled stomach of this strange woman, he was confused to see that she was heavily pregnant from the way she was gasping and wheezing. His eyes grew wide with shock.

"Ma! Come quick!" he shouted and helped the woman nervously inside. An angry face appeared round the crumbling kitchen door. "What on earth is it boy?!" she snapped, her fierce glove falling when she saw the woman. Mrs Saddlewick reacted quickly. "Ma –"Amelie cautiously began, but was interrupted by Mrs Saddlewick "Amelie! Fetch a blanket, and make haste!"

The next morning, the sky was clear and starlings and swallows sang in the trees outside the grim and fallen down Saddlewick house, and it was as if spring had at last grasped the world. For once, it was beautifully silent, and all was calm. But the night before had been immensely chaotic. The poor woman first gave birth to a cold, stillborn baby and secondly a shrieking premature new born. Not long after delivering the second child, the young woman died in the bundle of sheets, clutching her one tiny baby.

Mrs Saddlewick had tears in her eyes as she stroked the blue cheeks of the woman, nestling the still born into her arms and cradling the live child in her own. The woman's eyes were open and glassy, no life left inside them.

The next day the Saddlewick family took all their best clothes and laid the woman and dead baby in a cart, lovingly covered with black cloth. They laid the young family in the ground and buried them illegally in the ratty grave ground. A crow cawed in a skeleton tree then flew away. No words were uttered throughout the whole family, even the baby seemed to know.

Many years passed, and soon the Saddlewicks had taken the child in as one of their own, and the family were in peace for the rest of their lives.

The uninvited guest

Banshee the wild cat-Bengal leopard style

The uninvited guest

Toya Cleopatra was a scruffy, messy, filthy stray Siamese. She lived in Paris, prowling her territory below the Eiffel tower. She had a distinctive bitten ear and luminous emerald slitted eyes. She was not to be messed with in your wildest dreams. Toya was just licking herself carefully on the paw between the claws, a quite sensitive area, when she saw a school bus trundling slowly along, and she saw her chance. She sprinted as fast as she could to catch the bus and leapt onto the blindingly yellow vehicle and was suddenly engulfed by the excited shrieks of hundreds of eight year olds.

'It's a cat!'

'She's sooooo cute!'

'Grab her!'

'Wow!'

'Aahh!'

'Cute!'

One plump boy snatched her by the scruff of her neck with his greasy fingers and started ruffling her fur backwards. 'That's the last straw!' she thought to herself and she dug her claws into the fat boy's thigh.

'Owwww! She scratched me!' 'I am bleeding!' exaggerated the boy as she clutched his swollen leg between her claws. 'Serves you right!' Spat Toya, but of course he could not understand this, but he still got the message.

'Horrid kitty!' he taunted and all the little girls squealed.

'Hisssss! Back off! You meanies,' she hissed and all the children jumped onto the seats and burst into ponds of tears, as she came prowling around, growling at any one who dared put their feet down.

'Hey kids, are you alright in there? A cat is it? Tommy! Will you pick her up for me? That's a good boy.' called the driver from the front of the bus.

Nervously, Tommy picked up Toya, who he carried with shaking hands as she struggled, scratched and hissed to no avail. 'Ahhh, good little kitty!' he anxiously coaxed through gritted teeth as he firmly gripped the arched back of Toya.

As quick as a flash, Toya screeched loudly and scratched for her life in every direction, and suddenly she broke free. She ran as fast as she could, desperately hunting for anywhere to hide.

'Oi! Pussy come back!' yelled the bus driver as Toya jumped onto the luggage rack.

'Oh, all right you sour puss, but you better come down! You hear me?!' he threatened with a sigh. He continued to drive the bus erratically, leaving cars in his wake, honking their horns in confusion and anger.

'Mew!' Toya cried. The bus plodded slowly onwards, the children giving nervous glances at Toya every now and then, and Toya returned each one with a sly scowl. When at last they reached the school, a tall, plain, bland building armoured with vicious looking wired gates.

'Now I'll have some fun!' mewed Toya quietly to herself as she realised the bus had slowed down. With a thud, the doors opened. She slunk carefully off the bus remembering to scowl, while the children stared and screamed in horror as she squeezed her thin body between the barbed gates and into the school grounds, scratching herself badly in the process.

Soon she found herself in a boiling hot steamy corridor, and prowled proudly until she found the first classroom, which unfortunately for them was the nursery class. The door was slightly ajar, and if she swivelled her ears a tiny bit, she could just hear hushed voices from inside. The teacher seemed to be telling a story. 'And the tiger roared and made friends with Zebby the zebra. The end!'

whispered the teacher. 'Thank you Miss Fields,' chanted the children in unison. Toya chose this as her time to enter.

'Ahhhh! It's a real tiger!' squeaked the infants in terror. 'Now pipe down kids!' called Miss Fields as the petrified toddlers screamed. 'Now shoo, kitty shoo!' Miss Fields snapped angrily, shoving Toya out and slamming the door.

Toya licked her tail, as if nothing had ever happened. 'Now where shall I go?' she thought to herself, and as she pondered this, she found herself walking towards the assembly hall. 'Oh goody!' growled Toya as she soundlessly padded into the vast room. The teacher, a short, bald, fat man in a ridiculous suit seemed to be the Head teacher. 'And now, we shall discuss literacy and science Year Two.' he droned as Toya kept to the shadows, keeping herself well hidden. She saw her moment, as the head was bending down and couldn't resist the temptation. She leapt onto the Head's bottom and began howling an un-tuneful caterwaul. Naughty Toya! This caused such a catastrophe that almost at once Toya was expelled.

A chase ensued and the teachers chased her around the hall, as the children shrieked and pointed, attempting to grab the cat as it bolted past them. A bright young teacher decided to empty the class hamster out of its cage and crept up behind Toya with a make shift cat cage. 'Yowl, hiss' Toya screeched. Clang! The cage door slammed shut and Toya was taken away, never to be a wild cat again.

The wave

The wave

We were at the seaside and it was a hideously windy day, air was slapping our faces as we struggled against the wind. Granddad and I walked over to the side of the pier. I looked down to the rough waves crashing against its rigid Victorian pillars. Then I looked up to the screeching gulls, circling the harshly lit, bright shops for unexpecting victims to steal chips to hungrily gulp down.

I struggled to hide a suppressed smile as a bald, old and rather fat man plodded out of a greasy fish and chip shop, licking his lips greedily. The sight of the steaming newspaper parcel he loosely gripped in his sausage fingers was too much for the gulls. He was an easy target for them. In a flash a speedy seagull had zoomed in and pecked the chips out of his hands, caught the package and flew off again, cackling with glee as the man looked as if he was about to cry. Silly him- I knew I would never be stupid enough to make the same petty mistake. Even Granddad had to stifle a snigger as he pushed his spectacles back onto the bridge of his nose and pulled his anorak closer around him. He shivered.

" Beth, we really should be going now..." he mumbled.

"Yes, I know but can we just look at the waves a little longer?" I pleaded.

" Ok then" Granddad said doubtfully. I looked back at the waves, they seemed really angry. They roared in pain as they hit the scratchy stone wall beneath the pier and recoiled again, only to repeat the torture. "They really are getting rough." I thought to myself. I turned my back and leaned against the cold metal bars of the pier. I stared up at the steely grey sky and then I heard a noise like a stone being dragged across sandpaper but I shook off the thought as some old pier ride screeching into action... it was really loud now though. Granddad's eyes widened, he began shouting and pointing but I couldn't hear him. "What was that?" I yelled. He shouted louder but the noise deafened him. I rolled my eyes, Granddad often played tricks on me but then other people around me began to point too. Suddenly I guessed what was happening but it was too late- a millisecond after I began running the huge wave crashed down, soaking me to the bone...

Printed in Great
Britain
by Amazon

31626989R00025